A Christmas Book

Svend Otto S.

English version by Joan Tate

Pelham Books

What a hustle and bustle –
Christmas is coming and it's cold outside.

Everyone hurries through the streets to...

...the market to buy fruit and trees,
toys and a Christmas star.

As the people go in and out
of the bright shops, the hurdy-gurdy man
plays his Christmas tunes.

In the carpenter's workshop,
there are no more toys to make,
so all the shavings can be swept away.

The poet, too, has finished
his Christmas verses,
and now wonders who will read them.

Outside, in the cold,
the snow falls thick and fast...

...while at home, the tree stands ready by the stove,
waiting for the door to...

…open.
Everyone has come to see the tree…

...now bright with candles
and coloured hearts,
the star shining on the top.

The kitchen, too, is all hustle and bustle,
big pans steaming, good food sizzling…

...the goose already off to the baker's for roasting.

Out on the farm, the men have come in
for their Christmas dinner.
The cat, too, will have her share…

...and even the watchdog has been given
a double helping out in the yard.

All is quiet and peaceful until…

...the church bells ring out
and the lights glitter on the icy streets.

Inside, it's warm, and as the candles flicker,
some listen to the preacher, while others doze.

On Christmas Day,
the poor man whistles
for his pennies…

…while at home,
the party has begun.

Dear Lord, in a world of change …
… please leave Christmas as it was,
and let us all be children again.